The Nanny Diaries
#5
Jessie Madison

Chapter One

Nanny for Hire

DEAR DIARY,

I graduated college with a degree in child care and high hopes for the next chapter of my life. I had planned on working at a day care for a few years. It would give me real world experience to pad out my resume so to speak. I would have a fulfilling career that I loved. My income would allow me to finally move out of my parent's home, get my own place where I would live below my means, saving for my future.

I would begin to date seriously. I was sure I'd meet a few rotten guys, but there'd be some good ones too. I might get disappointed or have my heart broke along the way to finding Mr. Right. We'd get married and buy a house big enough for the family we'd plan on having someday. There would also be room enough for my in home daycare. This way I could stay home with my children while having an income. It's almost impossible to survive without a two income household in today's world.

That was the dream. No, it was more than that. It was a plan. It was what I thought had been a good, solid, strong plan. Then I graduated college, and the real world gave me a reality check.

I searched for months without being able to find a job. At least, I couldn't find one in my chosen profession. I was employed. I still had the job I worked all throughout college at the movie theater. It was only part time, but I could pick up a shift here and there. My boss was unwilling to give me a permanent full time position. I can't blame him really. He knew I'd put my notice in as soon as I found something else.

I had given up. I started to apply for entry level office positions. I had hoped to find something full time with benefits that would afford me a modest apartment. In the back of my mind, I had considered returning to school. It was difficult coming up with another degree that would complement my child care degree that wasn't teaching. And, of course, that was something I wanted to endure the classes to obtain.

Nothing against teachers. I respect them truly. I just don't think it's the job for me.

As I was rewriting my script and generating a new plan for myself, this job prospect fell into my lap. Literally.

I was sitting on a bench in the park, clearing my mind after yet another failed job interview. It was the last of the daycare interviews that I had lined up. No one from my office applications had called me yet. As with all my daycare interviews, it was the same story. Half of them wanted someone with working experience. How am I supposed to have experience if no one will give me a job to build it? The other half pointed out my education. Because I continued my education to get a bachelor's degree instead of an associates, they felt I was too over qualified for what they were looking for and couldn't afford me.

They most assuredly could afford me. I just needed a job.

Like I said, I was sitting on this bench when a man walking through the park threw his newspaper at the trash bin next to where I was sitting. He missed. It landed in my lap instead. The man yelled his apologies, but continued to walk on by.

I picked up the folded paper and moved to throw it in the

trash. I noticed it was open to the classifieds. Right there, in the middle of the page, bolded and outlined, was the ad for the Higgins' nanny.

I laughed. Loudly I might add. I probably looked like a lunatic to anyone around me. Why had I never thought of this before? I had been limiting myself to daycares, nurseries, and kids' club organizations, but I never considered being a full time nanny. I had also never thought to use print ads as a resource for my job search. I had completely stuck with online listings.

I had given up, but now I had renewed hope. It must have been fated. What are the odds? When I think about how the universe lines things up so perfectly, I am in awe. I had to be sitting just so on that bench that day. The stranger had to be walking through that particular park on a path that would take him by that exact bench at the time I was sitting there. He had to have a newspaper which is almost a thing of the past. It had to be opened to the classified section, folded in half, and folded in half again. His attempt to discard it had to miss and land in my lap perfectly with the side of the Higgins' ad facing up for me to see it. To add on top of that, the millions of other fated events going on all around the world at the same time, it truly is a wonder. I immediately called the phone number listed and set up an interview for the next day.

I thought the interview went extremely well. It was for a live in nanny at the Gibson estate. Higgins was Jenna Gibson's maiden name. I thought it was a clever trick for someone who didn't want to disclose how much wealth the family had to just everybody. It would help to deter anybody only responding to the ad for less than legitimate means.

I was wrong. It turns out Jenna Gibson is just a first class bitch. No, she's a cunt. No, actually there is no word strong enough to describe her, but I'm getting ahead of myself.

The nanny position was for two young children, both boys, ages four and six. It was a live in position with great pay. There were even benefits. I would have every Sunday and every other Saturday off, but my days off were subject to change based on Mr. Gibson's schedule. He would often travel for work and loved to keep these kids close which meant the nanny would travel with him. A passport was required, and luckily, I had one.

This sounded too good to be true, and it turned out that it was. It was a job that would pad out my childcare resume. It would help me save money for my future. And I'd still have time off for dating. The problem was the job didn't exist.

Mrs. Gibson's attitude toward me during the interview was promising. She liked that I had a degree and not just babysitting experience. She liked that I was young. I would be full of energy and not as strict as some of the older applicants seemed they would be. I walked out of that room confident the job was mine.

My confidence began to wean over the next two weeks when I never heard back from her. It sucked that I didn't get the job, but it only stood to reason a prize that sweet would have many people scrambling to win it. After two weeks, she called and offered me the job. She wanted me to come by the next day, but I would officially start next week.

I was to show up at 9 a.m. I would meet Mr. Gibson, get a tour of the home, meet the boys, and fill out some paperwork, and so on. It was all typical orientation stuff for a nanny position I presumed. I would be shown my living space then I could begin moving in with my first shift on Monday. I called the movie theater to put in my notice, not even sure if I'd be able to work it out. I packed up everything I thought I would need and half a bedroom's worth of stuff that I knew I probably wouldn't. I could barely sleep last night. I was filled with excitement over starting this new job.

I arrived this morning at 9 a.m. sharp and knocked on the door after getting through gate security easily. I rang the doorbell. Then I rang it again. The door was finally answered by a young man who appeared to be in his mid-twenties. "How may I help you?"

"Hi!" I said grinning. "I'm Jessie Madison," I introduced myself. "The new nanny."

"The what?"

"The new nanny," I repeated. "I'm supposed to meet with Mr. Gibson at 9 a.m."

He looked at me cautiously, but he opened the door and let me in. "Wait right here," he said. Then he disappeared through a doorway on the left. When he returned, he was with an extremely handsome man who didn't look a day over thirty. If that was Mr. Gibson, he looked young for his age.

Chapter Two

Temporary Nanny

THIS IS ABOUT THE TIME all hell broke loose. The young man I soon learned was named Travis. He was Mr. Gibson's assistant slash part time butler until the new one was hired. Even though I was in the room and present for the entire conversation as it unfolded, Travis would stop and give me an update as to what was going on every few minutes. It would've been comical if not for the awkwardness of the entire situation.

Needless to say Mr. Gibson knew nothing of his wife's intention to hire a nanny. He wasn't just surprised to see me; he was angered. Somehow, and for some unknown reason as to why I or anyone would go through the trouble, he thought I made the whole thing up. He began loudly ordering me to leave, or he'd call the police.

I agreed to leave, but mentioned I had the email from his wife with all the details of my new position. As I turned to head to the door, he demanded I show it to him. I did only because I don't like to be accused of anything I didn't do. I make my own mistakes plenty well enough on my own. There's no reason to add to the tally.

Once he saw it, he calmed down. Well, no, that's not entirely true. Mr. Gibson calmed his rage toward me, but he was still mighty angry at his wife for 'pulling a stunt like this as he put it. He barked out order after order. I felt bad for Travis having to scribble short hand and begin doing what he was told while still taking more notes. Meanwhile, Mr. Gibson tried to get ahold of his wife.

"If you wait a moment, Mr. Gibson will figure out something to compensate you for your trouble," Travis told me.

Like I didn't just hear the two of them discussing it.

Jenna was turning out to be a hard person to get ahold of and it only further irritated him. While waiting for his calls to be answered, he'd made snide comments to Travis about how she never liked those children, but he didn't think she'd resort to something so outlandish.

That one took me aback for a minute. To hear him say his wife never liked their children was quite a shock. As he continued, I picked up on the fact they were adopted.

"Lance and Levi are Mr. Gibson's nephews," Travis explained.

"Jenna!" Mr. Gibson practically screamed into the phone. "Where are you? We have a situation here. One that you caused I might add."

The way his voice so sharply cut through the entire room made me jump. I was thankful I wasn't on the receiving end of his anger.

"What do you mean?" Mr. Gibson took a few steps away.

"The airport? What are you talking about?"

This was sounding deep. I wondered if I should just try to slip out the front door quietly. Every time Travis glanced away from me, I took a sidestep toward the entry way.

"Your parents? For how long?"

Jenna Gibson hired a nanny for her to visit family. That's what it sounded like to me. I didn't know what his compensation was going to be. It could be anything from gas money to a hundred bucks just to get me out the door. I didn't need it that bad. I just hoped the movie theater would let me take back my notice. Not having a good, full time job wasn't nearly as bad as having no job at all.

"What! You're leaving?"

With that, Mr. Gibson disappeared through a doorway on the other side of the room. His voice still carried with a weird echo, but it was harder to tell what was being said. Travis hung behind for a minute or two before slowly following in the direction of where Mr. Gibson had gone.

It was my opportunity to make a run for it. I grabbed my purse I had set on a side table and went to the door. It was locked. I fumbled with the lock and finally got it open. Once outside, I made my way to the car, happy to be gone from the chaos going on inside.

There had been a tumultuous array of emotions ravaging inside of me since arriving. I went from the excited nervousness of starting my new job to being put on the defense from being accused of lying. There was the satisfaction of proving I was right and not up to no good. It was followed by the confusion of what was going on and what would happen. Then it ended with the shock of learning Mrs. Gibson hired a nanny to let her husband know she was leaving him. I felt embarrassed and humiliated for him.

My hand was on the car door handle when I heard Travis call to me. "Miss! Miss!"

I should've left. That is what a smarter person would've done. Instead, I looked up to see Travis approaching and waving his arm frantically.

"Miss," he said again, coming around the side of my car.

"Jessie Madison." I told him my name again.

"Yes, Miss Madison," he said. "You're leaving?"

"Uh, yeah," I said, shifting my eyes nervously. "It's just... Um..." I was tripping over my words horribly. "I felt like I should," I finally said.

He nodded. I could see by the way he looked at me that he understood completely. "It's not very professional." His words defied his eyes.

I took a deep breath. This was too much. I'd been here maybe twenty minutes at the most and didn't think I could whiplash through another emotion. Yet, I did. "Nothing about this entire morning was professional," I challenged.

"Agreed. It appears Mr. Gibson's wife has..."

"Left him," I said bluntly.

He closed his eyes and inhaled deeply. It was beyond me why I was the brunt of his frustration. He wasn't the one who was caught in the middle of a scene. "She is taking some time for herself," he said.

The corner of my mouth curled up, but I managed not to laugh. "Fine. She's taking some time."

"The point is," he said, waving his hand in the air, "we are in need of someone to care for the children short term."

"Short term?"

"If you're interested," he added.

I didn't know what he meant by short term. I had thought maybe Mr. Gibson was hoping his wife's departure would be rectified quickly.

"The issue of Mark's nephews has long been a problem area for Jenna," Travis explained.

I looked at him at the mention of Mr. Gibson's first name.

He noticed and corrected himself. "Mr. Gibson will be in need of a nanny for the children with the separation appearing to be permanent. He will be happy to employ you while he works toward filling the position, and he will honor the terms of the agreement you made with his... With Jenna."

What the hell did I just hear? "He wants to keep me on as the nanny while he finds a nanny?"

"Yes, exactly. He can't be certain how long the position will last, and you are welcome to stay here during that time. It wouldn't be necessary to move much in since it is only temporary," he said, glancing at the packed backseat of my car.

What he didn't know was that it was packed with the overflow that wouldn't fit in my trunk. "But it's already decided I will not be staying on long term?"

Travis smirked at me. "He wants someone with more experience in charge of the care of his brother's children."

"May I speak to him?"

"Mr. Gibson?"

No, the man in the moon. "Yes, Mr. Gibson."

"He would like to make introductions with you more formally at his earliest convenience, but he's in a video meeting with a client right now."

I could tell Travis was waiting for an answer. He probably spent more time with me already than he should have. He kept glancing at his watch every thirty seconds like it would magically rewind. "Fine, but I'm keeping my other job if this will only be temporary."

Travis opened his mouth to speak, and I could tell by his expression he was about to say that wouldn't be allowed.

I held up my hand to shush him. "It's part time evening. There will be no interference." I didn't give him the chance to object. I started walking back into the house.

It was Travis who gave me the tour, explaining the additional strain it was putting on him. He was Mr. Gibson's trusted assistant, but filling in as butler while that position was open. Now, he was tasked with giving me a crash course in the care of Mr. Gibson's nephews.

He finished the tour and had me fill out some paperwork. It was mostly tax forms plus a confidentiality agreement. "Mr. Gibson likes to keep his private life private," Travis said.

That's how I came to begging my theater boss to let me keep my job while sorting through my belongings to find the most absolute necessities to move in to my room. Every box or suitcase I brought into the house was met with a disapproving stare from Travis.

All of the plans had changed. It was Friday night, and I wasn't sure about even leaving my room. I had yet to properly meet Mr. Gibson or his nephews. Travis had said that would come tomorrow. I would begin working on Monday. I'm beginning to regret not asking if meals were included, but I'm not about to seek him out to ask.

Chapter Three

Downside

DEAR DIARY,

There hasn't been a day since I arrived here that I don't regret my decision to stay. Apparently, there's no hurry to find a new nanny. That's not entirely true. The importance is currently on hiring a butler. Mr. Gibson is extraordinarily picky about who he employs which I don't fault him for being that way. I still wish things would get moving. I hate being left out in limbo about my future.

Yes, I know I can quit. I could hand in my notice or just leave at any time. There are two reasons for me to continue my suffering here. One, I don't want Mr. Gibson preventing me from future employment elsewhere, and he seems like the type of person who is powerful enough to have that kind of pull. Two, I'm saving money. When I leave here, I should have the money in the bank to move into my own place as soon as I find a good job. It is helping propel my future plans by continuing to deal with this insanity.

Mr. Gibson makes it perfectly clear that he doesn't like me. It's rare for me to come into contact with him, but when I do, his disdain in present. He eyes my outfit, how I've dressed his nephews, what I'm feeding them, anything at all, really. No matter what the situation is, he will find something to criticize. It's like a constant reminder to me that he doesn't feel like I'm good enough for the job. Luckily, I don't have to tolerate it much, but it does make me uneasy when I see him.

That's completely unlike dealing with Travis who is constantly hovering, watching my every move. He does more than just watch. He likes to accidentally rub against me regardless of how much room he has to pass. He's always making ridiculous comments about my body. Yes, #MeToo movement. I get it. I've thought about it. Believe me. It wouldn't do me any favors. I'd find myself out of the house in an instant if I said something to Mr. Gibson. I'm sure of it.

Once I have the money for my own place, I'll start applying again. That's if I'm still here. If I find something, I'll put in my notice and go. Until then, Travis is no different or worse than the frat boys I saw every weekend during college. Right or wrong, I'm made of stronger stuff than what he's trying to throw my way.

It wasn't all bad. The boys were wonderful. Lance was in school all day, but Levi only went half a day. They attended a private school, so I had to drive them and pick them up. It freed up a lot of my time and made my job so simple. They were gone in the morning, so I did my running or made my appointments for that time.

I'd pick up Levi and bring him home for lunch then it was nap time. I could read, talk to my friends, or anything else. It was essentially free time only I had to stay close by.

We'd go get Lance after school, and my day would be almost over before I returned. Dinner was served to the family promptly at six every evening. I had to have the boys dressed for dinner and to the dining room on time then my day was over. The staff was served dinner in the kitchen. Well, served isn't the right word, but we could eat. Breakfast I ate with the boys since their uncle was already working. Lunch was just me and Levi. But, dinner? That's when I was forced to deal with Travis the most.

Some days I'd get a break. He'd be catching up on some work of his own, or he'd have plans. There were a few others in and out while I ate which helped, but I wished they'd eat in the kitchen like I did instead of fixing something to take with them. They were headed home, unlike me and Travis. He was staying there temporarily while he was filling in as the butler.

The sad truth is that he's very attractive. If he asked me out, I might've said yes, knowing my job was temporary anyway. If he flirted with me, I'd probably be responsive. He didn't do those things. Instead, he acted like he had a right to be crude and repulsive toward me.

I wasn't sure if it was because he thought he was superior due to his position. Maybe he felt like he was better than me because he was Mr. Gibson's assistant. It could be going to his head, and he felt like he was powerful by association. I also thought it might have to do with my tenure being limited. He knew I wouldn't be around long, so it didn't matter if he created a good working relationship or not. Of course, it could just be the fact I'm a young blonde woman, and he thinks I'm good for nothing more than getting his kicks any way he can.

Tonight, he took it a step too far. Not enough to make me quit, but enough for me to decide I would never suffer a dinner with him again. I'd order out, go to my parents' house, or just skip it all together.

I was already sitting down when he came in to eat. I always sat with my back to the wall because I don't trust him behind me even with a chair back separating us. It wasn't until he came into the room that I thought about the empty chair next to me.

Usually, it was loaded with bags and coats of the people on their way out to head home, but Travis was late. Everyone had left and taken their belongings with them.

Travis sat down next to me and pulled the chair close. It was roast chicken and mashed potatoes. He groaned as I took a bite, telling me he loved watching my lips wrap around the spoon.

I began to stand. I had enough to eat. Even if I hadn't, he made me lose my appetite. He followed me through the kitchen getting as close as possible, asking what my problem was as if I'd done something wrong. Then right before I left, he told me he had something I could wrap my mouth around.

In my room, I sat on the bed with the door locked. I watched the light coming in under my door, worried that he'd knock. I calmed myself and decided then that nothing about this place was worth dealing with Travis. I would start applying for other jobs right away. If I left before I had enough saved, I'd just have to go back to my parents' house for a little while.

After some time had passed, I relaxed and felt a little resolved about my decision. I took a long warm bath and soon all the anxiety and uneasiness washed away. When I laid down in bed, I took my relaxation one step farther.

I reached into my nightstand drawer and grabbed my small stim. It wasn't fully charged, but it had enough kick to the job. I played with my pussy and stuck two fingers inside of me as far as I could to warm up before bringing my hand up to my clit.

I tried to fantasize several times. As I thought about who I wanted to imagine bringing me pleasure. Travis' face kept flashing through my mind. It was annoying.

The stim made fast work of bringing me to climax. I gripped the sheets with my free hand and gently thrust into my hand as my toy vibrated and pulsated all around my love button.

I had to be quiet. The boys would soon be brought upstairs and put to bed in the room next to mine. In my head, I was screaming and moaning, *'Yes! Yes! Yes!'*

As my orgasm began to rock my body, Travis' face appeared behind my closed eyes again. I went with it. There was a sinister feel to my climax which made me cum harder.

When I cleaned up, I realized just how much I needed to get out of this place. I also needed to get laid. My body had been denied far too long.

Chapter Four

Fast Food & Fast Sex

DEAR DIARY,

It's Saturday, and I did have to work today. Just the same as during the week, I'm off at dinner time unless something comes up. Tonight I was free until Monday morning.

I had been on a dating app for half the week trying to see who might look good for a quick tryst. This particular app was primarily for hook ups regardless of the nonsense people put into their profiles claiming they wanted to find their soul mate. Everyone knew what everyone else was looking for on there.

Matt looked yummy. From the moment I browsed through his profile pictures, I knew he was the one I wanted to try on for size. He had been slow to answer which was disappointing. I moved on to my second choice and was making decent progress with him when Matt finally sent a message.

He had asked me out for Friday, but I couldn't make it. Mr. Gibson had a business dinner that night with clients from out of state which meant my shift didn't end when it was time to eat. It had to be this weekend that I had overtime. I was worried Matt wouldn't be free the next day or even find someone to scratch his itch while he went out with friends Friday night. Neither were the case.

I met him at a bar on Saturday because I wasn't about to have anyone pick me up here. Honestly, I don't even know how Mr.

Gibson would feel about it, and I'm not about to ask to find out. That was beside the point. I wouldn't want someone thinking they hit the jackpot with me and keep me around for the wrong reasons. This lifestyle wasn't my own, and it wasn't for long.

It was the first time I'd gone out since I started working at the Gibson estate, and it was long overdue. I had been nervous about meeting Matt. I wasn't a prude. I'd had one night stands before in college. They happened organically. I'd be at a party, run into a hot guy, and we'd wind up in bed together. I had never set out for the evening knowing hot sex with a stranger was on the agenda like this. How do you make small talk with a guy when your one pressing thought is imagining how big his dick is?

It turned out that I had nothing to worry about. The first beer hit just right. I didn't realize how stressed the circumstances at work had me until I was finally away from that environment and able to cut loose. One drink was quickly followed by another and another until I had to cut myself off. I didn't want to be too drunk to enjoy my much needed night of sex.

The alcohol also gave me some straight forward courage that I normally don't possess. I asked Matt outright, "You ready to get out of here and fuck?"

Nothing more needed to be said. He paid the tab and led me out the door. His hands had practically covered every inch of my body by the time we reached his car. Then the bomb dropped. "Can we go back to your place?" he asked.

Fuck. No, we can't go back there for multiple reasons, but I'm sure the main one would probably be I would get fired. I explained I was a live in nanny, so that was out.

"What about your place?" I felt hopeful, but I figured it was out. There'd be no reason to even ask me otherwise.

He started rambling about how he was living with his parents. Temporarily, of course. I didn't listen to most of his explanation. It was all excuses. We were young. What's so wrong about living at home until you're better established? While he was busy blaming a number of factors as well as other people for his current situation, I became bored and started losing my buzz. It was also a turn off.

"So what do you want to do? Car? Country road like when we were teenagers?"

Neither option appealed to him. "Well, I'm not shelling out the dough on a room when I don't plan on staying the night," I told him bluntly.

Instead of coming up with an idea, he got a look on his face that told me he thought the night was a wash. We were about to both go our separate ways, needs unfulfilled. That wasn't going to happen. Not on my watch.

"I got it," I said. "Get in." I walked to the passenger door of his car and waited for him to unlock it.

"Where are we going?" he asked. He didn't move from where he had been standing.

"Just get in. I'll give you directions."

Finally, he listened. We got in his car and pulled out of the bar's parking lot with me navigating our route. When we pulled into a fast food joint off one of the main roads in the city, he was a little disappointed.

"What?" He raised his eyebrow at me. "Are you hungry?"

I ignored the question and directed him where to park. It was along the main road, but away from the beaming lights that illuminated the parking lot. That end of the parking lot was also elevated about fifteen to twenty feet above the road. It wasn't completely out of view, but it wasn't in the direct line of sight either.

Matt pulled in and put the car in park. He turned to me, and I was sure he was about to question what we were doing there.

I didn't give him the chance. I leaned in for a kiss and climbed across the center console until I was barely balanced on it and one of his legs.

When he broke free, he asked, "Not here. You can't be serious?"

"I've rarely been accused of being serious, but why not here?"

He looked all around for people in the lot. No one was outside at the time. Then he peered out the windshield at the passing cars.

"Most of them will never glance this way." I tried to reassure him.

"Yeah, but..." he started to say.

"Do you want to fuck me or not?" I asked.

I guess the answer was yes because he pulled me close and began ravishing me, first with his hands then with his mouth. The foreplay was limited which was fine by me. I didn't need the warm up as much as I needed to feel my pussy crammed with cock.

Matt helped guide me over to straddle his lap. I hiked up my skirt and pulled my panties to the side while he pulled his jeans and boxers down far enough to expose his shaft. I lowered myself down and used the back of his seat to balance myself while he guided his tip into my tunnel. Once I felt him enter me, I came down hard. I was wet and ready. It had been far too long for me, and even the thought of sex had my pussy self-lubricating and ready for action.

I grinded my hips into him hard and fast. He fumbled with my top to expose my breasts and pulled them out of my bra one at a time. He massaged them while teasing my tits with his teeth.

In no time at all, I hit my first climax. My tunnel constricted around his cock, and I felt my cum pour out of me.

"Damn, Jessie," he moaned.

I continued to ride him. It was only about me in those moments. Matt was just the means to get what I needed. His hands moved from my breasts to my hips and back. Whenever he'd try to guide my movements, I ignored him and fought through to keep my own rhythm. I brought myself to orgasm after orgasm, not caring about anything but my own needs.

As I approached my fourth climax, I could tell he was getting close. I leaned close enough to gaze into his eyes and whispered, "Cum with me."

He listened like a good boy. I felt his buck and thrust under me while he shot his load. The tight walls of pussy massaged his cock while he released from the force of my own climax. I sank into his arms briefly while I caught my breath.

Afterward, the windows were fogged up completely. No one would've been able to catch a peep show for a while, but they may have seen the car rocking. We got a good laugh and cracked the windows to clear it up. We hit the drive thru while we were there knowing the poor workers were getting smacked with a good scent of sex when we were at the window.

Matt drove me back to the bar to get my car. He lingered a little too long in his goodbye. I thought we had an understanding going into tonight. This was about sex. No commitments. He told me he'd call, and I lied saying I'd like that. I knew I wouldn't be answering if he stayed true to his word.

I went back to the Gibson estate feeling so much better. My outlook on everything had improved. It's crazy how a good fucking sets things right.

Chapter Five

Busted

DEAR DIARY,

The bliss from my multi-orgasmic night with Matt was short lived. Mr. Gibson had seen me come in that night. I didn't think much about it. I walked in through the side entrance the staff was supposed to use and went straight to my room. He happened to be in the kitchen when I went through. I smiled and nodded to be polite. That was it.

I'm allowed to leave the premises. It's not like I'm a prisoner. Yes, it was late, but there was nothing that had ever been said to me about a curfew. It was something I actually asked when doing my paperwork. Travis explained I could come and go on my off time. I had a key and the code for that entrance. As long as I was respectful and didn't make noise if it was late, there wouldn't be a problem. That's exactly what I did. I walked up to my room as quietly as possible. No one would have known if he hadn't been standing in the kitchen when I opened the door.

Sunday was fine. I didn't see him all day. I did my laundry and hung out in my room mostly. I also caught up on my emails. When the nanny job posted, I applied for it. Mr. Gibson was somehow dead set against me filling the position. It could just be that I'm a reminder of his wife leaving since she's the one who technically hired me. I knew I wasn't going to get the job, but I figured the interview practice would be helpful.

There was an email that had been sent out late the previous week wanting to schedule an interview. Shoot. I thought I probably missed the chance. There was a link in the email that took me to a site where I could choose an available time. It would have to be in the morning when the boys were both at school. There was only one time slot left that would work, and it was Tuesday morning at 9am.

I selected it and filled out my information. When I hit submit, I waited on pins and needles until I got the confirmation email. I knew from what I heard from the other staff around the house that Mr. Gibson's secretary was handling the initial interview process. Basically, she was weeding the applicants and doing background checks to see who would move on to the second stage. It was perfect. I wouldn't even have to worry about Mr. Gibson being involved, but I would let her know I currently worked for him in that position. I figured she would mention it to him, and he'd request I be cut from the candidates.

Then all hell broke loose Monday morning.

I came down with the boys like I always do. They were dressed for school and had their backpacks ready to go. Once they sat at the table, I brought their breakfast from the kitchen. The cook had prepared bacon, fresh fruit, and toast for that day. It looked good.

When I went back in the kitchen to get my plate, Mr. Gibson was waiting for me. He asked to speak to me for a moment. Before I could say anything, he ordered the cook to keep an eye on the boys until we returned.

I followed him to his office. I didn't know what to expect, but I knew it couldn't be good, not coming from him.

He closed the door and motioned for me to take a seat across from his desk. When he sat down, he glared at me. He must know I applied for the permanent position. That's why he was mad.

"We need to discuss your extracurricular activities," he said.

"My extra... Oh." It took a moment, but I realized this was about my date Saturday night. There must be a curfew. If you're not going to be in by a certain time, then stay out till morning. That's what I thought was coming, something like that.

He nodded when it was obvious I was on the same page. "I understand my employees have personal lives. That's fine," he said.

"No, it's more than fine," he went on. "Of course they do, as they should. I just don't want it interfering with the goings on in this house and especially not with my boys."

I tried to speak, but he lifted his hand to stop me. I understood what he was saying. I would never do anything inappropriate.

"At any time, I could have clients here. It's rare, but there have been late nights entertaining people who could potentially bring sizable contracts to my company. I'm talking amounts you couldn't wrap your head around."

I looked down. I hated being made to feel like I was less than just because I wasn't wealthy.

"There's also the matter of my nephews. They can, and do, wake up during the night, leaving their rooms. Do you understand?"

"Yes," I said quietly.

"What do you understand?"

"I must always be professional in the house even when I'm off the clock."

He smiled, but it was unnerving. It was the smile of someone who had just caught someone in a lie or tricked them. "Exactly. I expect the next time you come in from a night on the town, and whatever," he leaned forward across the desk, "other extracurricular activities you may be participating in, you will check your appearance before coming in the house."

My mouth fell open, and I looked at him confused. I looked in the mirror when I went upstairs to my room that night. Other than my lip gloss needing to be refreshed, I looked fine.

"Miss Madison," he said, straightening up again. "Part of the back of your skirt was tucked into your panties."

My eyes widened. I was mortified.

"Your cherry red panties," he added, emphasizing he had, in fact, seen far more than I intended for him to that night.

If that wasn't humiliating enough, today didn't go much better. I hadn't seen Mr. Gibson since he dismissed me from his office yesterday morning, and I was thankful. It would be a long time before I could be in his presence without feeling uneasy after accidentally showing him my lacy panties. It was embarrassing, but I understand why he had to bring it to my attention.

When I woke up, I dressed up a bit more than I usually do for the interview. Then I carried out my duties like always with the boys. Once they were dropped off at school, I drove over to Brighten Industries which is owned by Mr. Gibson. My nerves grew increasingly uneasy along the way. I was nervous about the interview. Any job interview gives me anxiety. I've never been good at selling myself.

This job interview caused a lot more anguish. In the back of my mind, I worried Mr. Gibson would be upset when he learned

I not only applied, but was given an interview. I thought he would understand I only wanted the practice when I explained it to him, but now I wasn't so sure. The closer I got to his business the more I felt like I was making a big mistake.

Then after what happened yesterday in his office, I was afraid I would run into him while I was here. I figured the chances were slim. The building was huge. It was an entire city block and that didn't even count the multiple parking lots surrounding it. I didn't know until I checked in with security to get my visitor badge whether the interview would be held. It could be on the top floor near Mr. Gibson's office where I'm sure his secretary worked nearby or somewhere else. Even if it was, he'd be busy with meetings or phone calls. He might not even be in the building. I hadn't thought much about running into him until the last thing I wanted was for that to happen.

Security gave me my badge, and I waited in an uncomfortable chair for someone to escort me. A young woman called my name a couple minutes later. She wasn't Mr. Gibson's secretary; she was the secretary's assistant. Must be nice.

We walked to the elevators and went up to the penthouse. Funny. Even in an office building, that's how it was labeled on the elevator panel. At the top there was a button with the letters, "PH," over it. The woman briefly explained Mrs. Cartwright was ready for me, and she'd show me to the conference room. The rest of the trip was made in silence.

She opened the door for me, and I could see who I assumed was Mrs. Cartwright across the room about halfway down the long conference table. She stood to greet me with a smile, and I could see the table was arranged for the interviewees to sit across from her. I took a couple steps down the side of the table.

I didn't see Mr. Gibson in the corner of the room to my right. I didn't know he was there until he spoke.

There was a loud, "No."

I jumped and looked in the direction of where the voice came from. Mr. Gibson was tucked away with a portfolio note book on his lap. He was more hands on for this interview than I had been led to believe.

"You may leave, Miss Madison," he said sternly.

I was frozen in place for a moment. Then I heard Mrs. Cartwright say softly, "Thank you for your time."

I walked out of the room without making eye contact with either of them, but the tears were forming before I got back on the elevator. It was obvious I was fighting them back when I turned my badge into security. By the time I got to my car, they were flowing freely.

Chapter Six

Narrow Escape

DEAR DIARY,

I knew my boss would have something to say to me about the interview, and I was right. He sought me out that night to speak his piece. He was mad I even applied, and pointing out that no one at any time informed me I couldn't was not the smartest choice I ever made. It also didn't help trying to explain I only wanted the practice.

He reminded me that it had been made abundantly clear that I was not the right fit for this job, for his nephews, for his household. He claimed he was humiliated in front of his secretary, a woman who had worked for him since the day he leased his first office space in a strip mall. He demanded to know why if all I wanted was interview experience I didn't mention it to him beforehand. There were a number of open positions at his company at any given time that he could arrange interviews for if all I wanted was to sharpen my skills. Nothing I said was enough to calm his anger. My employment was temporary, and as far as he was concerned, it couldn't end soon enough.

After that, there was tension whenever we were in close proximity. It didn't have to be close either. I felt it during dinner in the kitchen just knowing he was in the next room dining with his nephews. It lingered when he walked out of a room I was in. I was sure it was noticed by the entire staff. It had to be. The only question was how much did they know.

Travis delighted in my discomfort. I guess he thought maybe since I was under enough stress from having pissed off the boss, I wouldn't take as much offense to his advances. It's hard to say what went on in his warped and twisted mind.

He doubled down on the amount of times he tried to cop a feel. Part of that was from increased opportunity as well. I no longer received emails or texts from Mr. Gibson himself reminding me of something in one of the boy's upcoming schedules, or alerting me I'd have to rearrange my days off because of an event I'd be needing to attend to care for his nephews. He cut off all communication with me. Instead, he passed the buck to Travis to fill me in, and he made sure to relay everything in person. It was a ploy to try to sneak a feel, touch me as he passed by, or brush my ass or tits supposedly on accident.

It was disgusting. I had already wanted my job to end sooner than later due to that heel, but now I wished for it. I hoped every day was the day it would be announced my replacement had been hired.

Then, Travis caught me in the laundry room yesterday on my day off. I was immediately on defense and a little afraid. He had shut the door that I always leave open, not that it mattered. There was nobody home, but us. Mr. Gibson had taken his nephews out to lunch, and the staff had Sunday's off unless there was something special going on which there wasn't.

It was just the two of us, and he was leaning against the door that was my only exit. I would literally have to go through him to leave.

"Thought I'd find you here," he said casually.

I did my laundry every Sunday afternoon. I had since I

arrived. He knew my schedule. This was the first time he had an opportunity like this to corner me. I wondered how long he'd been planning it.

Ignoring him wasn't going to work. It wasn't like I could argue I didn't know he was there when I turned to face him after he opened the door. It also wouldn't pass to pretend I couldn't hear him. The laundry room was big compared to most households, but it wasn't that large.

"Laundry," I said, trying to play it cool. "Fun stuff."

"I hear the spin cycle can be nice."

I stiffened and turned back to switching out my clothes. I put them in the dryer, trying to carefully conceal any under garments from his view as I did. I had never been fearful that Travis would ever do more than be a creep who made me uncomfortable, but he never had opportunity before either. I wasn't so sure anymore.

"You don't agree?" he asked, moving closer.

"What?" I tried to play it off.

"The spin cycle," he repeated. "It's too bad we missed it."

That was it. I'd had enough. I spun to face him. "That's it, Travis. I don't like it when you talk to me like that."

He laughed. "Is that right? Well, what do you like?" He stepped closer and brushed my hair behind my ear. "You like hooking up for sex with strangers you just met and coming home half dressed? We can arrange that if you'd like."

I could feel the redness flood my face. Mr. Gibson had told him. Part of me felt like it might be normal for someone to be open and honest about everything with their assistant, but part of me felt betrayed. Whether or not Mr. Gibson was in the right to let Travis know what happened, I didn't like that he did.

"Leave me alone, Travis," I said coldly.

"Or what?" he asked.

I couldn't move. I could barely breathe. My heart was racing with fear. He was right next to me. His entire body was pushed against my side. I could feel his hard on through the thin dress slacks he always wore.

"Just leave," I told him softly. My voice failed me.

"What're you going to do? Scream? Who would hear you?"

With that, I pushed him away and tried to make it out of the room. He grabbed me by my hair and arm and pulled me back. "Like to play hard to get, do you? I like to play too. My favorite game is taste testing."

Travis wasn't very big in stature, but he was stronger than me. He knocked me to the ground and kept pushing down on me with the hand that was wrapped in my long, thick hair. He unzipped his pants, and I tried my best to get free.

His cock was on my face. He was trying to pry my mouth open, but I clamped it shut tight enough I tasted my own blood from my teeth cutting through my lips. He pinched my nose until I had to open my mouth to gasp for air. When I did, I twisted away from him. I could feel a large lock of my hair being ripped from my head. I screamed.

It was just noise at first. Then I screamed again. This time I yelled for help. I managed to scream a third time, "HELP ME!"

Then Travis stuck his dick in my mouth to shut me up. I bit down hard. It was his turn to scream.

He backhanded me across my face then slammed my head into the washing machine. I was dizzy and felt like I would vomit. The door opened. I was confused. He wouldn't leave, not now. He'd make me pay for biting his dick.

There was a commotion and a lot of yelling. When I could finally stand without the room spinning, I realized I was alone. I pulled myself up and left the laundry room, taking a broom from the corner as I went. It was the closest thing to a weapon I could find. Once in the hall, I saw Mr. Gibson over top of Travis. I could see by the marks on his face that Travis had already taken a few blows.

I dropped the broom and ran to my room as fast as I could, locking the door behind me. I didn't know what to do. Leave? Shower? Cry myself to sleep? Exhaustion from the ordeal chose the third option, and I collapsed on my bed.

Later, Mr. Gibson came to my door with two uniformed officers. Travis had already been arrested, and they'd taken my boss' statement. He had heard me screaming when he returned home with the boys. He ordered them to go to his office and shut the door then he raced in the direction of my voice. All that was left was to take my statement.

Today, he gave me the day off with pay. He met with me in his home office first thing to see how I was doing. It was a completely different side of him than I'd ever been introduced to before. He was soft and caring. Mr. Gibson couldn't have apologized more if he tried. It all came out. I told him how Travis had acted toward me from the beginning, and I confessed how I was afraid I'd be let go if I said anything since it seemed like I had been skating on thin ice since the day I first arrived.

Mr. Gibson apologized to me. He hadn't told Travis about the night my skirt was out of place, but he was probably eavesdropping while we talked. He apologized for not realizing how hostile a work environment it had been for me. He also apologized for his role in that since he never gave me a proper chance.

He assured me things would be different going forward if I chose to stay although he wouldn't blame me for leaving. The staff would eventually find out what happened. Travis' arrest would be public record. The details of the charges would get released. Even if they kept my name out of the news, the staff would put two and two together.

I'm not entirely sure why I stayed. The only reason I can think is because I believed him and because he saved me.

Chapter Seven

Allergies and Offers

DEAR DIARY,

It's been crazy around here since Travis lost his job. That's how it's always referred to. If any of the staff have figured out what happened yet, they aren't letting on that they do. I had a few marks on my face. They weren't too bad, and I could easily cover them with makeup.

The butler was hired and has begun working at least. This was when it was supposed to get easier around here. There was still the matter of hiring a new nanny, but at least I was here to fill in until then. With Travis' departure, there was now an assistant position open. It made for a nightmare.

It didn't take long to fall in step with the rest of the staff, preventing Mr. Gibson from losing his mind. Everyone pitched in to keep him on track and focused. It was obvious how important an assistant was to him. He was so busy it was surprising he had time to wipe his own ass, let alone remembering to shake it at the urinal.

By the end of the week, I was taking my lead from the others and checking his schedule every morning to help keep him on track. Mr. Gibson had completely softened and was a whole different person in his interactions with me ever since the night he came to my rescue.

For the first time since learning about how his wife set him up, I was disappointed I wouldn't be staying. The job had provided what I wanted. It was giving me experience, and I had enough saved to move. Not only that, I could buy a little to help decorate the place once I moved in. With everything that happened with Travis and Mr. Gibson's change of heart toward me afterward, I had no doubt he'd give me a good reference.

Last night, I happened to come back in the kitchen after dinner. I went to my room, but I was antsy. I couldn't explain it. Normally, I kick back and watch TV or goof around on my phone. It was different. I couldn't sit still. It was like I had to go. I didn't know where or why, but I had to get there. That's the only way I can describe it.

Eventually, I decided to wander downstairs and find a snack. Maybe if I felt stuffed, it would act like an anchor to keep me still. It was almost time for the boys to go to bed which Mr. Gibson did himself. He had the same idea as I had because when I walked in, he was raiding the fridge, and the boys were sitting at the table.

He greeted me and joked about how dinner must not have been too filling if we were all gathering around the same time to eat again. I leaned against the counter and waited for him to finish first. The truth was I didn't come down because I really needed to eat. It was because I had to get out of my room.

Then it happened. Mr. Gibson pulled a tray of devilled eggs from the fridge and set one on each of the plates that were in front of his nephews.

"What are you doing?" I asked a little too loudly. In an instant, I took the egg off Levi's plate. Some of the yolk mixture had smeared on it, so I snatched the plate too. I set it all on the counter and grabbed a clean plate to replace it for the poor child.

Meanwhile, Mr. Gibson was questioning what I'd done.

"He's allergic to eggs," I said. He had to know that. He took the kids out to eat a lot. He had to know what they could and couldn't eat.

"No, it's peanut butter," he assured me.

"Eggs," I repeated, staring at him. "There's a reason the cook almost never fixes eggs for breakfast."

That made him pause to think. He cocked his head to the side, and the slow realization began to cross over his face. "That's right. My brother was the one who was allergic to peanut butter."

He hung his head, and I could tell he was really upset. I would be too if I had almost made a mistake like that.

Once again, the universe had lined up perfectly to put me in the exact right spot at the right time. If I had come down earlier, I might not have been there to see what he was about to feed his nephews. If I had been any later, it would have been too late. The only reason I went into the kitchen was because of the unexplainable urge to do something, go somewhere, and I couldn't explain why I was feeling that way.

"It's okay." I tried telling him.

"No, it's not," he insisted. "If it weren't for you, the ambulance would be on its way, and I'd be praying the epi-pen would be enough until the EMT's arrived."

Mr. Gibson glanced at the boys then held a finger to me to wait. He quickly offered them cookies which they eagerly accepted. Then he ushered me into the hall.

"I mean it," he told me privately. "You quite possibly saved his life. I owe you."

I shrugged. "We're even," I said. One corner of my mouth pulled up in a failed attempt to smile.

He nodded. "Yes. Even," he said.

Today, he pulled me into his office yet again. Instead of immediately assuming the worst, I thought it might have something to do with what happened in the kitchen and the eggs. I was wrong. It shouldn't have surprised me.

"The nanny position has been filled." Mr. Gibson said as soon as I sat across from him.

It knocked the wind out of me. I knew it was coming. I was never given an exact time frame, but it shouldn't have shocked me as much as it did.

He was still speaking, and I glazed over for most of it. Luckily, I caught the important parts. The new nanny would officially begin on Monday, and I would stay on for two weeks to help her transition. It wasn't for her sake, but for the benefit of his nephews because he knew they adored me.

A cleaning crew would be coming later that day to thoroughly sanitize my room. It was nothing personal. This was standard when anyone moved out. I knew he was being honest. The same had been done after Travis' family collected his belongings from his room. I would have the morning off of nanny duty to move into Travis' room. It was easier in the long term. The nanny needed to be near the boys.

After my two weeks, he was willing to give me a severance of a month's pay. "I'm sorry your experience here hasn't been a pleasant one," he said at the end.

I started to object, but just like the first time he called me to his office, he raised his hand to stop me.

"I'm not just talking about Edwards," he said, referring to Travis by his last name only. "I know I wasn't exactly a picnic myself. I made no secret about what I thought your potential as a nanny would amount to, and I apologize."

I smiled and nodded. I didn't know what else to say.

"It's a testament to your strength however. A lesser person wouldn't have stayed. It would have been too much for them to handle. After what you were subjected to at the hands of Edwards, I'm surprised you ever came back to work. I really do regret my part in what you suffered through."

"Thank you," I said. "It means a lot."

Mr. Gibson took a deep breath. "It's because of your experiences here thus far that I don't have high expectations for what I'm about to offer."

Chapter Eight

Walk in the Park

DEAR DIARY,

I'm not entirely sure, but I think Mr. Gibson only offered me the assistant position out of guilt. He didn't know how Travis had been treating me. I never said a word. Maybe that was part of it too. Maybe he realized he made my work environment feel so fragile that I didn't feel safe reporting what was going on with him. Somewhere, there was a part of me that knew this was somehow wrong like he was simply covering his own ass. I knew I should leave.

There was one thing that made me eagerly accept the position: travel. It had been mentioned by Mr. Gibson's estranged wife in my interview. That was what I had considered to be the biggest perk of working as the nanny.

When Mr. Gibson offered me the job, he mentioned that there was an upcoming European business trip. The first destination was Greece. It was in my top five list of places I wanted to visit. On top of that, the assistant would have more free time overseas than the nanny, so this really worked out to my favor.

It wouldn't hurt to keep working for him a little longer. Things could be entirely different now that Travis was gone for good. I may even like the job. The pay and benefits were great. Honestly, the only reason I would have to look for something else would be my dream of an in home daycare. That was the biggest downside. It wouldn't build my job history to help with that.

In the end, I decided to give it a try in the name of Europe. The assistant doesn't normally live in the house. Travis only did because he was covering two jobs at the time. Mr. Gibson decided I could continue to live on the property until I found my own place. I could go home and stay with my parents, but I figured I'd have more freedom if I stayed where I was. I love my folks, but they still treat me like I'm twelve.

I'd be able to afford a decent apartment on this salary, but there'd be time to start looking. It would be a couple weeks before I fully transitioned from nanny to assistant. One week later, I'd be on an international flight. The housing search would begin when we returned.

I had my first full weekend off in-between my job change. I went out with friends Friday night to catch up. It had been far too long since we really got to hang out like that. Come Saturday, I knew I needed another hook up. I didn't want to make a habit of having one night stands, but I also didn't have time to start dating with the trip right around the corner. Getting a good fucking to relieve some stress sounded great with everything that had been going on.

Once again, I found some eye candy on my dating app and met up with him. This guy insisted on dinner which I wouldn't bat an eye at normally, but I wasn't looking for a relationship right now. When I messaged him on the app, I made it clear I was looking for a fling before traveling overseas. There would be no worry whatsoever of me trying to come back for more than what he bargained. Most men would have loved that. Evan, not so much.

When he suggested dinner, I had that feeling like a void in the pit of my stomach. It just didn't sit right. Why go through the effort of paying for dinner, even if we split the bill, and making all that idle chit chat just to have steamy hot sex and walk away? I didn't listen to what my body was trying to tell me. I went ahead and met him.

Throughout the meal, I did get the unmistaken proof he was looking for more than a hookup. Still, I didn't panic. I figured I'd just let him down while I was putting my clothes back on to go home. We ate and went to a nearby park, the same one where I found the nanny job in the newspaper to be exact, for a walk. By this point, I was feeling frustrated in more ways than one.

While we walked, I waited until the perfect moment when no one was close enough to hear. I lowered my voice to be safe just in case and asked if he wanted to go back to his house. The look on his face was beyond comical. It was like the year was 1943, and he had been working up the nerve to ask to hold my hand or something. If he would've shown me his promise ring and told me he was saving himself for marriage, I wouldn't have been surprised given the reaction he gave me.

"Look," I told him. "I made it clear when we messaged earlier that I was looking for a hook up."

"Yeah, but I didn't think you meant it."

Are you fucking real? It's bad enough most guys think no means yes, but even yes means no now. "Why would you think that?"

"Just my experience," he said. "I've had girls say that before, but it never happens."

I chewed the inside of my cheek and took a good look at

him for the first time. He would be great to date. He looked exactly like the type of guy you'd want to bring home to meet the parents, not the type of guy you'd fuck against a brick wall in the alley behind a bar. That was probably most of the problem right there.

"And in these past experiences, did you do like you did with me? Take the girl to dinner and treat her like she was on a date? Or did you meet her somewhere sleazy for a drink then leave to fuck the shit out of her elsewhere."

Evan gulped. It was like a scene from a movie. There was a definite gulp caused by his nerves that was both seen and heard. I had made him uneasy with what I said.

"I'll be honest with you, Evan. Tonight was great if I was looking for a relationship, but I'm not. Tonight makes me feel like if I fuck you, I'll have a sad little lap dog following me for weeks, like I'll have to block you on everything then block someone else's account and phone numbers too that you use to reach me just to get rid of you. I'm not trying to be mean, but you're not acting like someone who is interested in sex."

"Oh," he said nodding. "I am interested in sex."

"I mean only sex."

He shifted his weight nervously and looked around at everything but me. A man was jogging near us, and Evan waited for him to pass. "Yes, only sex. I know. Is that supposed to mean I still can't treat a woman right beforehand?"

I thought the point of cutting to the chase was to, well, eliminate the chase. "No, Evan. There's nothing wrong with treating a woman right. Next time, tell her you plan on fucking her senseless, but you're going to buy her dinner first."

"Next time?" he asked, growing even more uneasy.

"Not with me," I laughed. I looked around at our options. The other side of the park would've been better, but I could make do. "Do you see that stone bridge over the creek?"

"Yes."

"On the other side of it is a bench that sits directly in front of a very large oak. Know where I'm talking about?"

"Yes."

Something told me this would be his first time outdoors. "I'm going to walk over there and wait by that tree. If you want my mouth on your cock, you will follow me."

When I said the word cock, he shifted his weight again, and I knew my words made his manhood move. His dick was standing up to see who was talking about him. "If not, I'll sit on the bench and offer myself to the first man who passes. But one way or the other, I'm getting laid tonight."

I took off across the grass as a short cut to the bridge. I knew Evan wasn't following. At least, he wasn't right behind me, but I had hope he'd show up. When I got to the tree, I looked back at the bridge. It was a decorative brick structure that stood at six feet higher than the path at its tallest point. As soon as I realized Evan was nowhere in sight, I saw the top of his head as he walked up the far side of the bridge.

In a minute, he was in front of me. "Where to?" he asked.

"What do you mean?"

He looked confused. "I thought you wanted to go somewhere for sex."

"I do, and I did," I said, walking around the tree. There was a small bare area back there. The only reason I knew this was because I was in the park one day when city workers were landscaping and pouring mulch. They were trimming too, and some of the guys were hot. I hung around and watched for a bit, wishing I could take them all on at once behind this very tree.

Evan laughed, but it was to try to hide his fear. He followed me though. "Someone might see us."

"They might," I said, unzipping his slacks.

He craned his neck in every direction. "What if we get caught?"

"What if we do?" I asked, freeing his semi-erect shaft from his pants.

It wasn't dark yet, but it was getting later. If someone walked by, they'd see Evan for sure the way he was standing tall behind the tree. They may just think he was taking a leak, not that it would be much better. We'd hear someone coming down the path before they reached us.

I knelt in front of him, and he chuckled again. This was out of his comfort zone, but he wasn't trying to stop me. It didn't take much for his semi to become fully hard and eager for attention.

He soon forgot all about keeping lookout, not that he needed to do it anyway. I moistened my lips and took the tip in my mouth, sucking gently. Each time I lowered my head, I swallowed a little more length until I had him entirely in my mouth. When I pulled my head back, I would glance up at him, but he had his eyes shut tight with his head tilted back.

I sucked him for several minutes while reaching my hand between my legs to start my own fire. I hiked up my skirt and slid my fingers down my panties. I rubbed my clit, keeping time with the work I was doing on his cock. When I was at the brink of climax, I stopped. It was time for Evan to finish the job.

I stood up, shimmied my panties down and off, putting them

in my purse. I leaned against the tree. Evan joined me immediately. He kissed my mouth then ran a trail down my neck and across my cleavage. I circled one leg around his waist and pulled him closer. It took a minute to get our balance, but he was soon gliding in and out of me, cupping my ass with his hands to hold me in place.

His cock filled my tunnel, and the excitement that came from the threat of being caught tripled my pleasure. I reached orgasm after orgasm much to my surprise. For a minute there, I wasn't sure Evan had it in him. It didn't take long before his shaft engorged inside me, and I knew he was ready. We didn't need a lot of time. I just needed something to scratch the itch before traveling overseas where I wouldn't even know the language, and this definitely hit the spot.

When we finished, Evan started asking about if he could see me again. It was tempting to tell him I'd hit him up when I returned, but I didn't want to make plans that far ahead. I definitely didn't want to answer questions about where I was going or why. I told him I'd be pretty busy for a stretch, but I'd think about it even though I knew it would be a no.

I got home to the Gibson estate late, but not past the rules late. I came in through the side door, but stopped in the kitchen to grab a snack to take up to my room. I knew I looked alright. I had checked my appearance several times before leaving my car and again before going into the house.

It didn't make a difference. Mr. Gibson came in before I left, and his face was screwed up in disapproving judgement. I wondered how he knew this time, but I didn't have to think about it long. I had my back to him, and I felt him touch me. It made me jump. When I turned around, he was holding a piece of tree bark he had picked off my shirt.

I would definitely be moving as soon as we returned from Greece even if it meant going home to my parents before getting my own place. I took the bark from him, and said, "Thanks. I was looking for that." Then I grabbed my stuff and headed to my new room with Mr. Gibson's exasperated face staring after me as I went.

Chapter Nine

To My Rescue Again

DEAR DIARY,

Mr. Gibson made it perfectly clear that when we returned from Greece I was to find a new living space immediately. That's not to say I had to move out the second we returned, but I had to find a place. It didn't seem like anything different than we'd already discussed except now there was a lot of anger and judgment in his voice when he spoke. I didn't know what his definition of immediately meant. I could start looking right away, but it could take weeks before I found something. If he got mad that I was taking too long, he might just fire me and be done altogether. I decided I would be moving back home while I looked for my own place.

When we were on the plane, I began to regret every life decision that led me to this point. Mr. Gibson had yet to get over his attitude from the night I came home with a piece of bark on my back. He never asked what I was out doing, and I certainly didn't volunteer the information. I could've had a few drinks with friends then fell and sat against a tree while laughing too hard to stand right away. I know this scenario is plausible because it's happened to me before.

His private jet was large, and it was sectioned off between where the two of us sat working and where the nanny stayed trying to keep the boys occupied. They had left in the morning, so that put a lot of work on the nanny. Once again, I was thankful not to be the one handling it. The boys came in for meals and to see their dad before napping.

Mr. Gibson did have me jot a few notes to type up, compose a few emails, and other assorted things along those lines. Primarily, the two of us went over his schedule with a fine toothed comb. He wanted to squeeze as much work as possible into these three weeks. His contracts in Greece were very important to him. It made my heart sink until I learned she wouldn't have to be present for all of it. In fact, I wasn't present for most of it.

Greece was amazing, and I had so much time to roam and take it all in as a tourist. Normally, I would stay closer to Mr. Gibson throughout the day, but he felt like that wouldn't be necessary for this trip. I'm still learning the ropes of what to do, and he wanted me to be comfortable in my actual position before throwing how to do my job in a foreign country at me.

As I toured the ancient city of Athens, I had my laptop in my bag just in case. Throughout the day, I would send reminders to Mr. Gibson of where he should be and who he was meeting with next. If he needed anything like a particular document, I used my hot spot to connect the laptop and sent it to him. It only happened twice during the three weeks we were there.

I was about to write that the men were so different there, but of course they were. Back home, I could walk down the street no problem. Occasionally, a guy might make eye contact and smile, but that was pretty much it.

This was definitely not the case here. I was complimented constantly. Most of the men hitting on me wore wedding bands which was eye opening. Sometimes, a man would stop and try to chat. One guy even ran up to me with a small bouquet of flowers that I refused to take. It was flattering, but very unsettling at the same time. The worst part was they were very handsy. Almost every one of them touched my arm or shoulder. Some would play with the strap from my bag which was very near my breast. One even put his hand on my waist while talking to me. It stopped me from venturing too far from the hotel at night.

That's not entirely fair. I had no more fear of these men than I did the men back home. If I'm being entirely truthful, I probably had more fear back home because I know the risks there. Here, I have no idea how common it is for a woman to be attacked. I tried to look up the statistics, but every website said something different.

The thing that worried me was not knowing my surroundings. If I was in a situation where I needed to flee, I wouldn't know where to go. I don't know where anything is located. I can't get back to the hotel without the GPS app most of the time. I wouldn't know who to trust to help me. Attacks can occur anytime of the day, but I felt a little safer when the sun was out.

On our last night in Greece, Mr. Gibson took me out to dinner. He had scheduled a lot of time with his boys while we were there, and it was supposed to be a dinner for all of us. However, his last meeting of the day was running very late. It was an important one. He had already renewed contracts, but this was to bring in new business. He had to stay until the work was done.

The nanny went ahead and took the boys out to eat. I thought I'd tag along, but Mr. Gibson asked if I would wait. I agreed before I knew how long it would take. I was starving by the time he was free. I snacked a little bit while I waited, but I was afraid of becoming too full.

I'm so glad I didn't overdo it. Dinner was amazing. I had really missed out by coming back to the hotel so early every day. When we walked outside, I realized I had left my purse at the table, and Mr. Gibson went back in to retrieve it. While he was in there, a random guy on the street started to hit on me.

I didn't understand the language well enough to know every word he said to me, but creepy doesn't need translation. I had packed one exquisite dress in case I wound up needing it for work, such as a business dinner, which I never did. It was my last chance to show it off, so I wore it tonight. The dress was read satin, strapless, and it had a matching wrap. This guy kept toying with my wrap.

He'd tug at it and try to pull it off, or least down where he could see my cleavage. He grabbed the ends and threw them up over my face. While I pulled them back down, he walked around me and smacked my ass. It was mortifying. I kept repeating to leave me alone and that I was waiting on someone. Yes, I said the word no multiple times thinking he might at least recognize that word if nothing else. Either he didn't understand English, didn't believe me, or flat out didn't care.

We weren't alone on the street either. Others were coming and going from the restaurant, or waiting on a car. No one did or said anything. I knew Mr. Gibson would be back out in a minute, so I wasn't too worried. It was just humiliating having this guy act like a tool, treating me like this while the only thing anyone did was enjoy the show. It would be even worse when my boss reappeared. Some assistant I am if I can't even take care of myself.

Then he was there, right beside me. He yelled at the man in

his native language, so I couldn't follow everything that was said. Then the man started speaking perfect, albeit heavily accented English. That asshole knew what I was saying the entire time.

Mr. Gibson berated him for not knowing how to treat a lady and told the man to leave me alone. The man, of course, defended himself by saying I was a single woman, and as such, he had the right to hit on me. They argued until Mr. Gibson lunged at him prepared to strike. During the whole ordeal, Mr. Gibson told the man I was in a relationship with him. I knew he only said that to help get the man to back off, but it still came as a shock to hear the words.

We made our way back to the hotel in silence. I couldn't wait to get there. I was crawling out of my skin with anxiety. This was not the way I wanted my boss to remember me in Greece. I wanted him to realize how valuable I was even if I wasn't present with him. This was our last night. This would be his takeaway.

In the elevator of the hotel, I knew I had to say something. I started to tell him I was sorry.

"Sorry?" he asked. "For what?"

"For the scene at the restaurant," I explained. "I'm sure you think I did something-"

He cut me off. "What kind of person do you think I am, Jessie?"

His words caused my heart to skip a beat, and I sucked in my breath. He had never called me by my first name. Hearing it, in that tone, sent an electric current through me that found its way to my clit in record time. Mr. Gibson was a very attractive man. I'd have to be blind to not notice that, but I had never thought of him in any way other than my boss. That changed. I wanted him, and I wanted to take him right there.

He was staring at me like he wanted an answer. "I just mean with the other nights at the estate," I began. I wasn't really sure how to explain it. "And then what happened with Travis," I said.

"We don't need to speak of his behavior unless you'd like to, but I don't see how that has any bearing on what happened tonight," Mr. Gibson said.

I shook my head, not wanting to discuss any of it anymore. I was really regretting having said anything at all.

"Please, Jessie," he said gently. "Why did you feel like you needed to apologize for what happened?"

"It's been my experience that the woman is typically blamed for not having behaved appropriately," I said.

"For asking for it?"

I nodded.

"I guess I don't behave typically because I certainly don't blame you, but why would you think that of me?" he asked.

I wasn't sure if he was genuinely hurt that I did, but that's how he sounded. He may just want to improve how he acts for the benefit of his company. The elevator doors opened, and we walked toward our rooms which weren't far away.

"Because of the nights I went out. I know you disapproved of me and my... activities. Maybe you thought I flirted, and it got out of hand," I explained.

"Well, I did not," he said.

When we arrived at my room, he said goodnight and reminded me of what time we would leave for the airport tomorrow. We weren't flying out in the morning this time. It was a later departure, but we had to be checked out. Our luggage would be taken to the airport and loaded on his jet. I'd still have hours to hit any last spots I wanted to take in before I needed to head that way myself.

I unlocked my door while he walked away, but he stopped before I entered my room. "By the way, Jessie," he said, without turning around, "I didn't disapprove. I was jealous."

Mr. Gibson continued walking to his suite and let himself in without another glance in my direction. I know because I stared at him with my mouth on the floor the entire time. I couldn't believe what I heard. Jealous? Of me being with other guys? It wasn't possible. It isn't possible. There's no way that's what he meant. It had to be he was jealous of not having anything tying him down and being able to live more carefree without the responsibilities that came from running a massively expensive business and having children. That must be it.

Chapter Ten

Mile High Club

DEAR DIARY,

I had been wrong once again. He meant exactly what he said. He was jealous of the guys I was spending my time with.

Apparently, he had been interested in me since day one which was the real reason he didn't want to hire me on as the full time nanny. It wasn't because it was too cliché to have an affair with the nanny, but because he didn't want to have an affair at all.

His wife had just left him, and he already knew the problems that arise when you try to juggle a woman with business. One of the two always suffers. For him, it will be the woman every single time. His business was too important to him. He figured when I was out of the house, things would return to his iron clad focus on expanding. Until then, I was an unnecessary distraction as much as he wanted to act on it.

Then, Travis happened. It really opened Mark Gibson's eyes to how he felt for me. It had gone from a deep sexual lust to true feelings without him realizing it. When he walked in that night and saved me, he had to fight the urge to take me into his arms and shower me with kisses while holding me tight to him. He wanted to apologize for not being there and make promises that he'd never fail me again. He couldn't though. Not only did he know it wasn't his fault, but there was nothing between us except a cordial, at best, working relationship.

The way he felt afterward was just as much a surprise to him as it was to me when he finally told me. The feelings he had only began to grow. He found it hard to stay away from me. When we did have those run-ins that showed him I had someone taking care of my physical needs. It made him insanely jealous. That's why he had said something the first time. He didn't want to see proof that another man had what was out of reach for him. He began to regret not having acted sooner and started to feel like he missed his chance with me.

All of this came out on the plane while I lay in his arms during the flight home. I listened to him spill out his heart and soul feeling like I was in a dream. This was too good to be true. A man like Mr. Gibson, Mark as he asked me to call him, didn't fall for young nobodies like me. I've gotten way too far ahead of myself.

I met the private jet on time for the flight. In fact, I was quite a bit early like usual. We all loaded up and had dinner almost as soon as the plane was in the air. The boys hung out for a little while sharing stories of their Greece adventures with their dad and showing off pictures. Some of these tales had been told to him before. I had heard most of them several times already too.

The nanny took them to their section of the plane to tuck them in for bed. There would be jet lag to deal with when we returned, but the Greece clock dictated it was past their bedtime.

It was soon after that I asked about our sleeping arrangements. I had barely flown before, never first class, and certainly not on a private jet. The chair I was sitting in would be more than comfortable, but I didn't know where I was supposed to lay down.

"You're not even going to bring it up," Mark said, sounding disappointed.

I knew he was talking about the comment he made the night before. Part of me wanted to bring it up. The word jealous had been screamed inside my head on repeat the entire time since he boarded the plane, but I didn't know what to say about it.

"I was surprised to hear you were jealous," I said. It was simple and to the point. Most importantly, it was the truth. If he wanted to continue the conversation, he could because I didn't know what to do except possibly to strip in front of him. He didn't seem like the type of guy who was looking for someone so forward.

Mark nodded slowly and clasped his hands together. "I can see that. I developed quite a strong poker face in my line of work, and I can't turn it off in my personal life."

I didn't say anything. I hoped he would continue, and he did.

"I'll lay all my cards on the table, Jessie. I want you and for a lot more than just sex."

My mouth dropped open, but I couldn't respond.

"You have time to think about it. In the meantime," he got up and showed me the options for sleeping. There were small bunks that I could choose from. I'd fit easily, but they were narrow.

"Or," he said, pulling back a curtain to reveal a much larger bed. "You can join me if you'd like. The choice is yours."

I stared at the bed for a minute, knowing instantly what I wanted. I lifted the sun dress off over my head, revealing my near nude body to him. I removed my bra and slid my panties down to my feet, kicking them off. Then I climbed into the bed and laid down under the covers.

He pulled the curtain and left. I must say it was not what I was expecting, and I almost laughed at myself for being such an idiot. He was offering me to share a bed with him, not join the mile high club.

A minute later, he returned, pulling the curtain shut tight. "Sorry about that," he said, stripping his clothes off quickly. "I had to make sure there would be no interruptions."

I bit my lower lip and watched him undress. I always knew there was a muscular body under all the suits he wore, but he was more than I had imagined. As soon as the last piece of clothing hit the floor, he and his eight inches of hard cock joined me.

Mark came up behind me and pulled me tight to his chest. One hand roamed between my legs while his mouth crushed down on my neck. His hand spread my legs open, pulling the top one up and over him then his fingers found their way to the outer folds of my pussy.

I could feel him position his shaft between my legs, and I started to move to an easier access position. He put one hand on my shoulder to stop me and used his other hand to guide his cock inside me.

I whimpered as he entered me. His hard member felt amazing as it tore me open.

"That's it," he whispered. "Keep it down. Can't let the whole plane know what we're up to."

He thrust in and out, building momentum each time. I bucked back into him, keeping in time to his movements. When my first climax exploded, I griped onto his upper leg and squeezed tight to release how I felt without shouting it out loud.

That's when he flipped me to my stomach. He straddled me and entered me from behind, keeping me flat on the bed. It felt amazing. With each hard thrust in, I felt my body inch forward from his strength. I buried my face to stifle my moan and came several more times.

I lost track of how many times I climaxed, but after one of my orgasms, he slowed his movements. He began pulling completely out and reentering me again which was both bliss and torture. Then he pulled out and pushed the knob of his cock against the hole of my tight ass. I tensed up, and he asked if it was okay.

The truth was that I was scared out of my mind. I knew it'd hurt, but I was curious too. Finally, I nodded and whispered, "Yes."

"I'll stop whenever you want me to," he said.

Mark spit onto my hole a couple times then repositioned the knob at my entrance. He leaned forward, slowly pushing his cock into my ass. A searing hot pain ripped through me, and I felt like he was splitting me in two. I didn't say anything to stop him because I wanted to take him.

He continued to push forward, and the pain eased just a little bit. He pulled out and repeated the process several times until he had finally fully entered my ass. I couldn't believe I had taken all of him.

He took my hand and slid it underneath my body, ordering me to play with my clit. I did as I was instructed. Mark began fucking my ass, slow at first then building to a fast momentum that had me screaming into my pillow.

I came again. I could feel the walls of my pussy trying desperately to convulse and constrict around something, only to find my tunnel empty. Not long after, Mark came inside my tight ass. I felt his hot cum paint the inside of my walls then he collapsed next to me.

He pulled me close, and it took several minutes for either of us to regain our composure. We fucked several more times during that flight. Each time was better than the previous. In the wee hours of the morning, we stopped to rest. He pulled me close, telling me how he truly felt about me.

The plane will be landing soon. I'll wait for the nanny and the boys to leave before I even think about getting off my chair. I'd rather as few people as possible be witness to how difficult it is for me to walk right now. Once I return to the Gibson estate, I will be packing my things to move again. I won't be going far. I'll be moving into the other wing, into Mark's room, and I can't wait for our next adventure.

Coming Soon

Stay tuned for more of the Nanny Diaries and Family Secrets series by Darling Coxx! The third installment of the Family Secrets series is expected February of 2022!

More by Darling Coxx
Nanny Diaries #1

Lacey Moore bit off more than she could swallow when she took the position at the Wyndham estate. What was supposed to be the perfect job accompanied by great hours, pay and perks like living rent free in the guest house soon turned out to be more than she had could have ever imagined. The main duties of her job included making sure the entire staff stayed satisfied, and it was a job she intended on doing well.

Nanny Diaries #2: Vicki Sweet

Vicki Sweet didn't know what she was walking into when she took the job as nanny for the Rayburn's. Soon she found herself loaded with maid duties as well as chasing after the children while Aidan worked and ignored all of his wife's illicit activities. Tori Rayburn needed to be put in her place, and Vicki was just the woman for the job. Chasing after Tori's affairs, Vicki began stealing them away one by one, but her eye remained on the ultimate prize. Vicki would have her saucy way with Aidan before her job ended, and once she set her mind on something, she always got what she wanted.

Nanny Diaries #3: Mindy Cummings

MINDY CUMMINGS DIDN'T except anything from Mark Jacobs expect a decent paying part time nanny job that worked well with her college schedule. The apartment over the garage for her own private affairs was an added bonus. She soon learned how little she knew about the man she'd been babysitting for since she was a teen. It wouldn't take long to realize that his touch was the one thing she needed more than anything. Fantasy after fantasy, he filled her thoughts. His face was who she envisioned no matter who she was with. The one thing she didn't expect was for fantasy to become reality.

Nanny Diaries #4: Sierra Bottoms

Sierra was left scrambling when she found out her parents had nickeled and dimed her college fund dry. She had never had a job. Her parents told her that school was her priority. Now, she was going to have to work while attending a junior college if she had any hope of achieving her goals. The biggest problem she faced was keeping her legs closed while on the clock. When she was hired as a nanny by Mr. Bridges, sex wouldn't be a problem because he could barely stand the sight of her. Or was it his way of hiding the true lust that burned inside?

Family Secrets: Lexi's Education

Lexi had lived a sheltered life thanks to her step-dad. He was a good man, a good, muscular, handsome, type of man. One thing he made sure of was that no one took advantage of his gorgeous step-daughter. Soon she'd be off to college in another state where she'd be at the mercy of the boys she met on campus. She needed a different type of education, a sexual education, and her step-dad was the right man for the job.

Family Secrets: Tiff's Fantasy

Tiff's life was far from perfect when her mom wrecked it even more by moving the man she was about to marry and his son into their home halfway through senior year. Connor was not a complete stranger to her. She'd known him all throughout school, and the fact he was about to officially become her step-brother was a nightmare. The most popular boy at school and the least popular girl under one roof. The only thing that could make it more complicated was her fantasies about him and his attraction to her.

About the Author

Darling Coxx is a seasoned writer who has been featured in many major publications under her given name. Taking a break from interviews and personal experience pieces, she is trying her hand at short novellas in the same genre she's been working in for most of her life.

Her adult entertainment career began while working as the manager of an adult store. It is her favorite position of any she's held, before or since. It was there where she made the contacts that allowed her to venture into the world of adult entertainment both in her own writing as well as producing a few pieces of her own.

Please feel free to reach out to her at DarlingCoxx@gmail.com. Follow her on Instagram @DarlingCoxx to stay updated on future publications.

9 781952 422232